Who Left the Light On?

To Saweta and to all the bright architects...
—R.M. & A.M.

This edition is published in honor of Mary Katherine Dingman Tegeder

First Published in France in 2015 by © Éditions Frimousse
Translation rights arranged through the VeroK Agency, Barcelona, Spain

First Restless Books hardcover edition November 2018

Hardcover ISBN: 9781632061898
Library of Congress Control Number: 2017944638

Cover design by Jonathan Yamakami

Printed in China

1 3 5 7 9 10 8 6 4 2

Restless Books, Inc.
232 3rd Street, Suite A111
Brooklyn, NY 11215

www.restlessbooks.org
publisher@restlessbooks.org

Who Left the Light On?

by Richard Marnier

Illustrations by Aude Maurel

Translated from the French
by Emma Ramadan

Restless Books
Brooklyn, New York

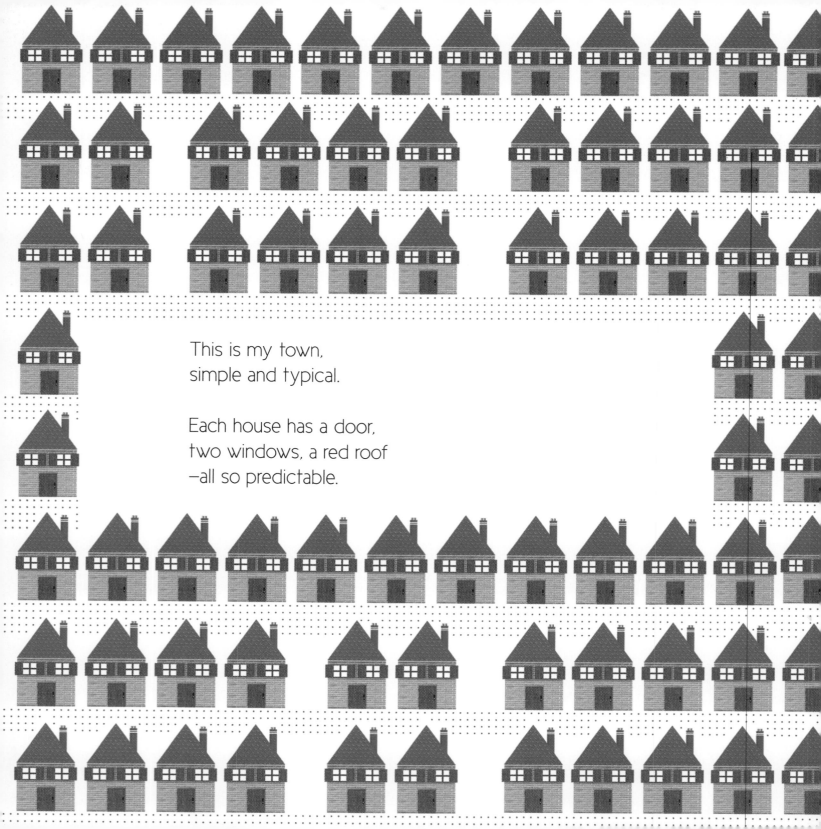

This is my town,
simple and typical.

Each house has a door,
two windows, a red roof
—all so predictable.

Each door has a handle and a lock that shuts tightly.
Each window has gray shutters framing it nicely.

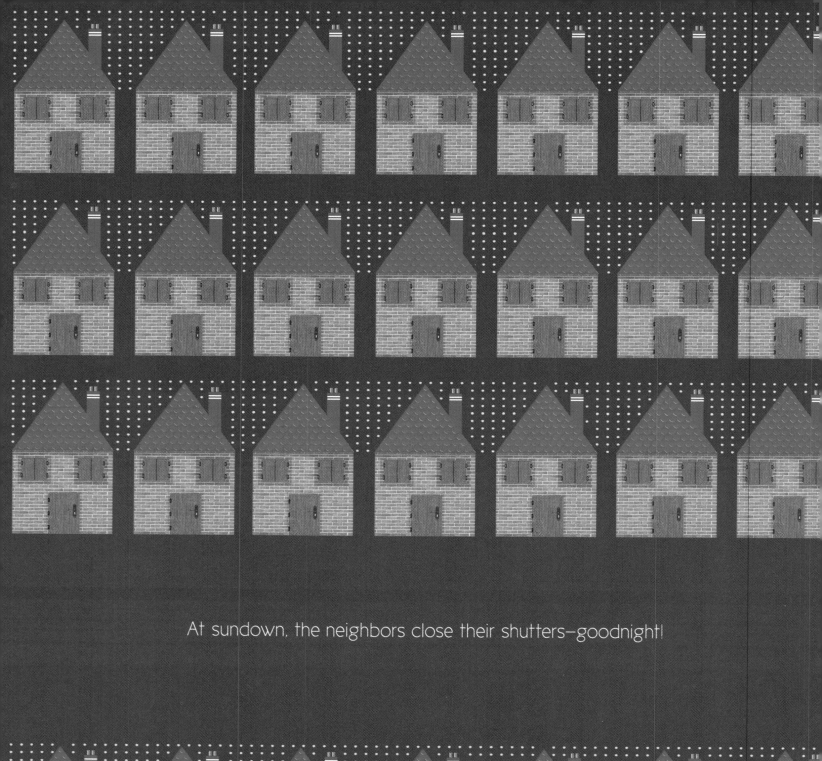

At sundown, the neighbors close their shutters—goodnight!

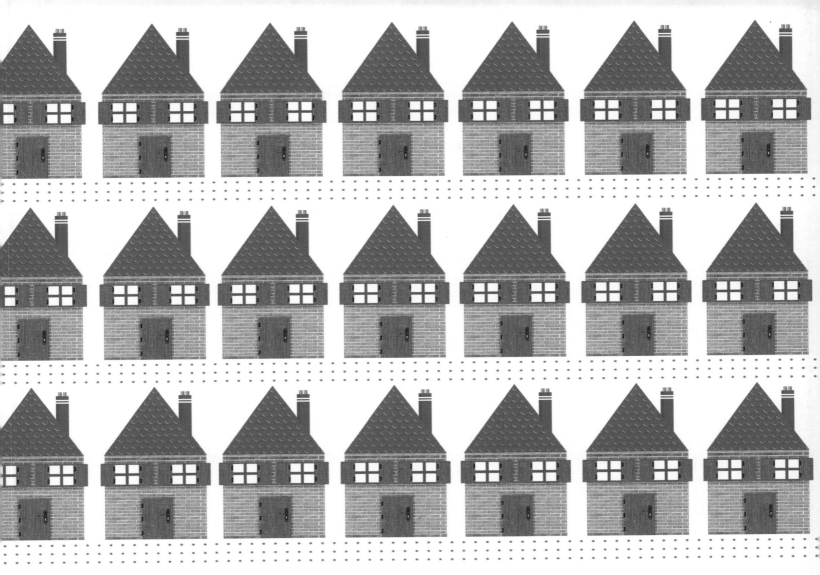

At daybreak, they open them—oh so polite.

But then one night... someone leaves on their light!

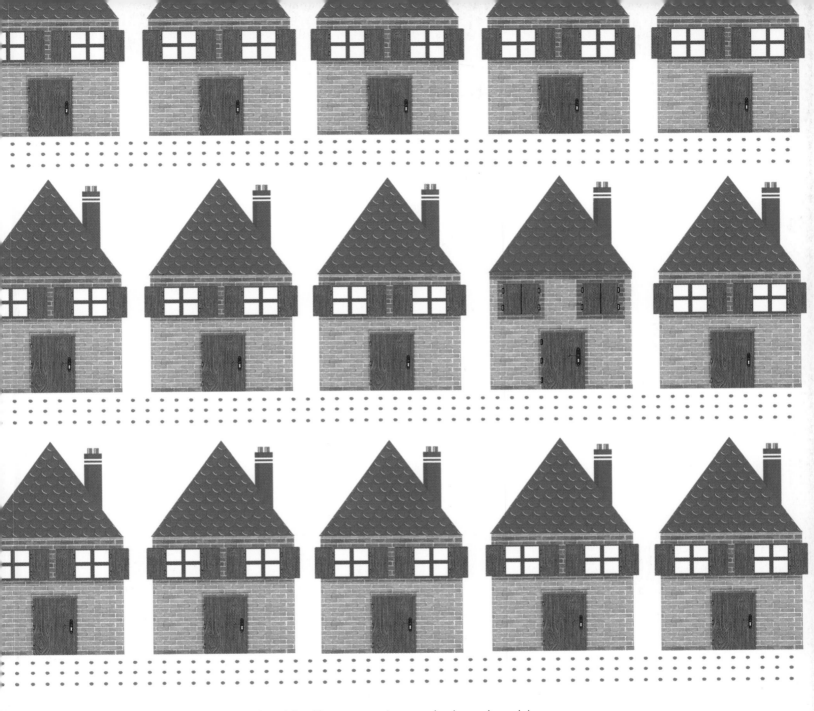

And in the morning, what a shock!
The shutters are sealed tight!

After days and nights of this irksome behavior,
the neighbors begin to whisper and wonder.
Who is that who lives next door?
We've never seen anything like this before!

Thankfully, one fair afternoon, that nuisance sets out for some faraway place....

What a relief for the town, but what a disgrace!
The house, abandoned by all, starts to collapse.
The roof starts to leak, the walls have huge cracks,
and the dangling shutters are beginning to flap.

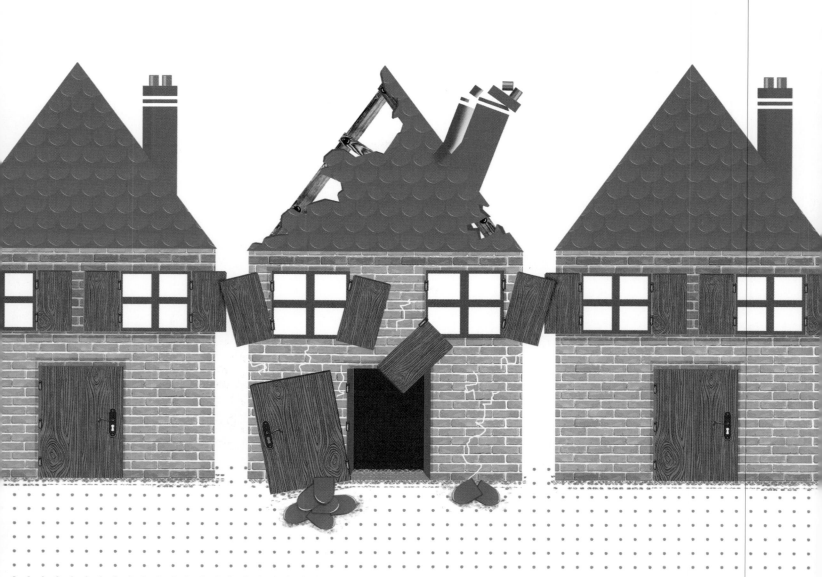

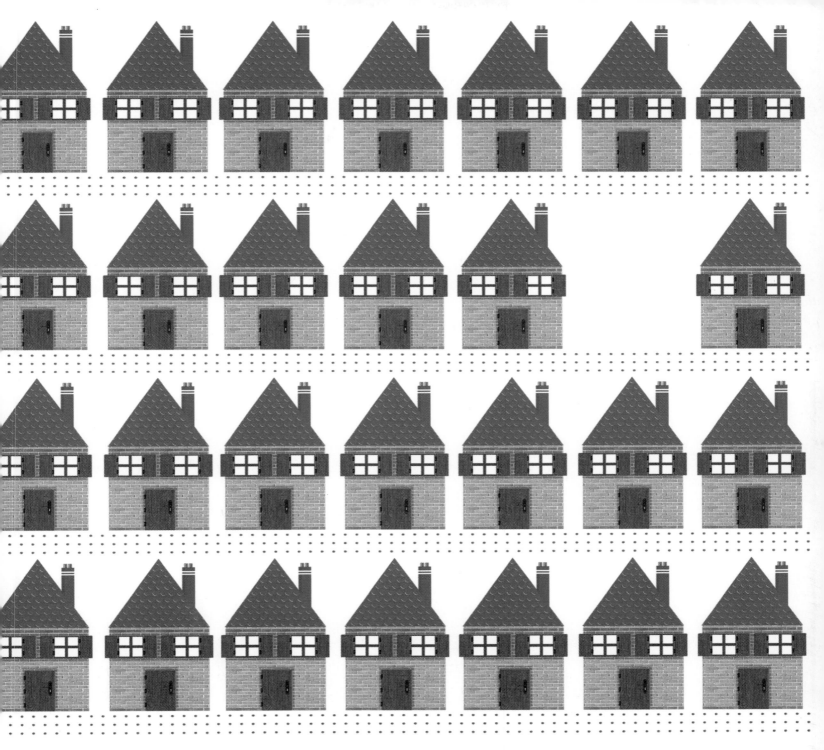

The house gets so bad, the town has it demolished....

One day, the traveler returns and finds all abolished.
No trace of the home but a large empty space.

So, with everything gathered from time on the road
the oddball creates a brand-new abode.

It's a comical house that stands out on its row.

All of the neighbors cry out in dismay.
Did you see those colors? What awfully poor taste!

But then a neighbor decides on the very next day
that blue-painted shutters look more than okay.

Nearby, a neighbor does shutters in red—
and finds this bright color is better instead!

Another one adds a turret outside
and a tower on top that's quite dignified.

Someone builds higher, not one floor but two,
plus a stable below and a wall of bamboo.

Next door a neighbor adds a deck to the roof
and an open-air bathroom that has a great view.

Across the street, there's a house made of sticks,
while their neighbor prefers windows to bricks.

Astonishing concrete chalets,
wooden forts,
marble huts,
castles of lace,
flower towers,
and birthday-cake estates.

Each day,
a thousand ideas blossom,
a thousand fantasies take shape,
a thousand projects are underway....

In the neighborhood now, you'll be sure to admire
round roofs, spiral stairways, a rocket-ship spire,
rusted-steel walls, drawbridges, a hat with a spider.

There are homes with one story,
while others climb high.
Some houses ornate—and others sedate.

In this town of invention,
there's no such thing as perfection.

Every grownup and child
lets their fancy run wild,

inspired in each innovation
by the one who left the light on.

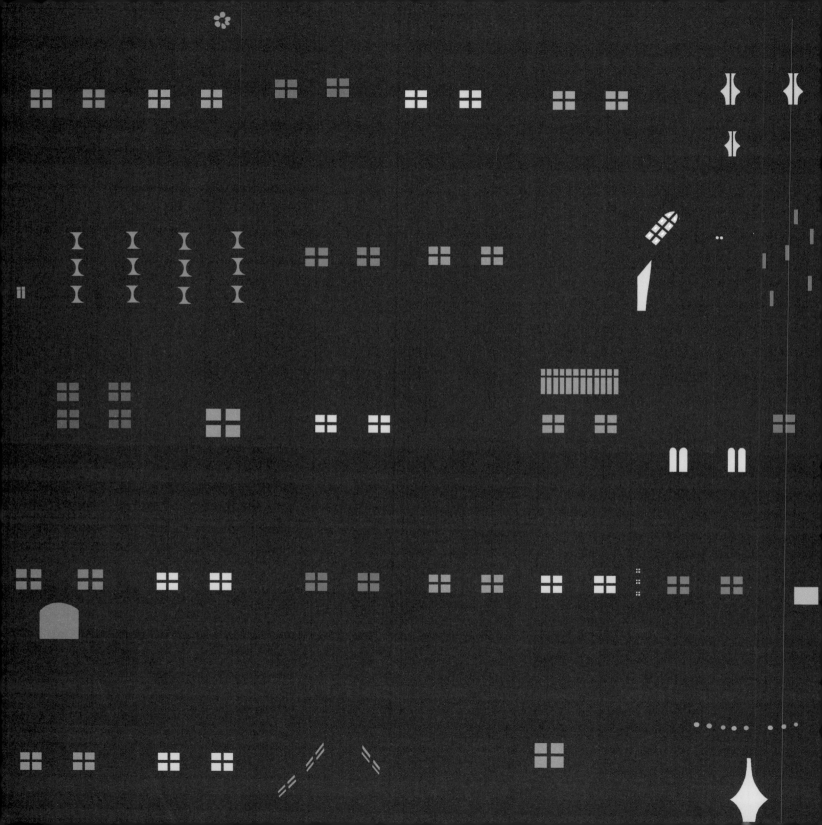

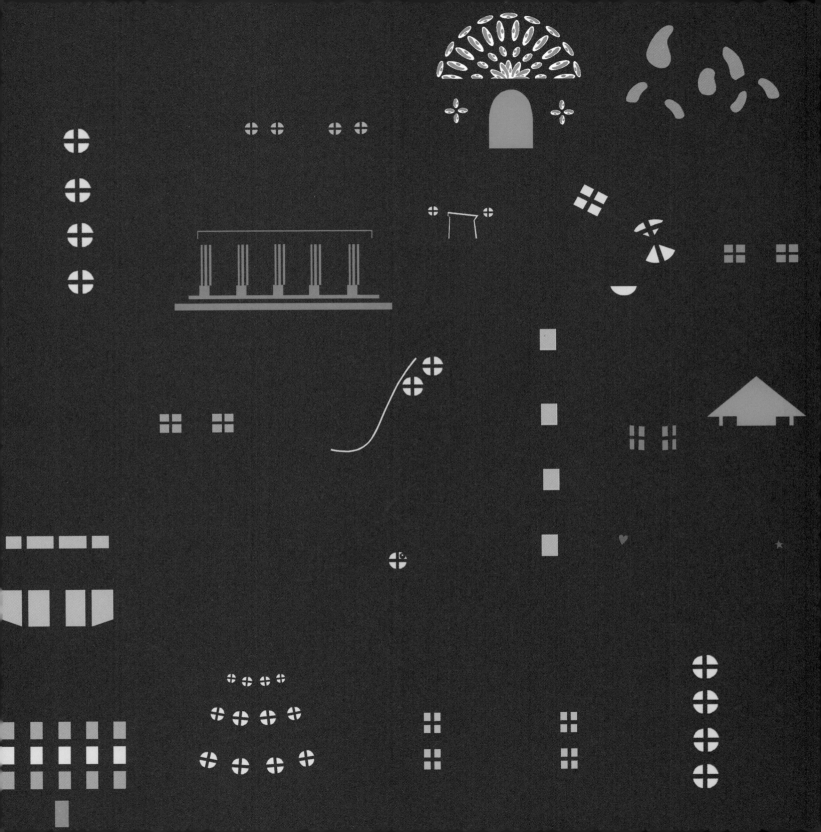

ABOUT THE AUTHOR

A former student of visual arts, Richard Marnier is a writer and an artist. In his work, he mixes sculptures, drawings, and design with the conventions of writing and visual arts. Adept at children's stories, he has published several books with the Éditions Seuil Jeunesse, Les P'tits Bérets, Éditions Frimousse, and Éditions du Rouergue.

ABOUT THE ILLUSTRATOR

A former student of the prestigious École Supérieure des Arts Appliqués Duperré and L'École supérieure des arts décoratifs de Strasbourg, Aude Maurel has collaborated with Franco-German TV channel Arte. From animated film to still images and illustrations, she now creates her own children books, sometimes collaborating with her partner, author Richard Marnier. Aude likes to assemble words together, end to end, turning them into necklaces. She has thousands of stories to tell, some of which will become illustrated books.

ABOUT THE TRANSLATOR

Emma Ramadan is a literary translator based in Providence, RI, where she is the co-owner of Riffraff, a bookstore and bar. She is the recipient of an NEA Translation Fellowship, a PEN/Heim grant, and a Fulbright scholarship.

ABOUT YONDER

Yonder is a new imprint from Restless Books devoted to bringing the wealth of great stories from around the globe to English-reading children, middle graders, and young adults. Books from other countries, cultures, viewpoints, and storytelling traditions can open up a universe of possibility, and the wider our view, the more powerfully books enrich and expand us. In an increasingly complex, globalized world, stories are potent vehicles of empathy. We believe it is essential to teach our kids to place themselves in the shoes of others beyond their communities, and instill in them a lifelong curiosity about the world and their place in it. Through publishing a diverse array of transporting stories, Yonder nurtures the next generation of savvy global citizens and lifelong readers.

VISIT US AT RESTLESSBOOKS.ORG/YONDER